NICKI WEISS

SUN·SAND·SEA·SAIL

GREENWILLOW BOOKS 🕮 NEW YORK

GOUACHE PAINTS WERE USED FOR THE FULL-COLOR ART.
THE TEXT TYPE IS ITC USHERWOOD.

PRINTED IN SINGAPORE BY TIEN WAH PRESS
FIRST EDITION   10 9 8 7 6 5 4 3 2 1

LIBRARY OF CONGRESS CATALOGING-IN-PUBLICATION DATA

WEISS, NICKI.
SUN SAND SEA SAIL / BY NICKI WEISS.
P.   CM.
SUMMARY: A FAMILY PICNICS BY THE SEA
AND ENJOYS SWIMMING, EATING, PLAYING,
AND WATCHING THE SIGHTS.
ISBN 0-688-08270-X.
ISBN 0-688-08271-8 (LIB. BDG.)
[1. BEACHES—FICTION. 2. PICNICKING—FICTION.
3. STORIES IN RHYME.]   I. TITLE.
PZ8.3.W425SW   1989
[E]—DC19   88-16391   CIP   AC

FOR
LISA
ERIC
AND
AMANDA

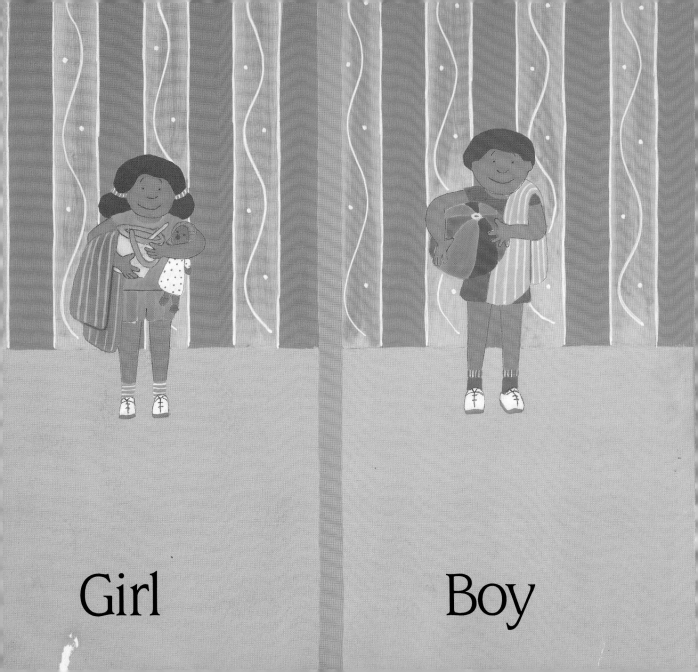

Girl   Boy

Sister   Brother

Man   Woman

Father   Mother

Fruit   Sandwich

Pickle Jar

Basket   Swimsuit

Beach Ball   Car

Road   Sky

Cloud   Pine

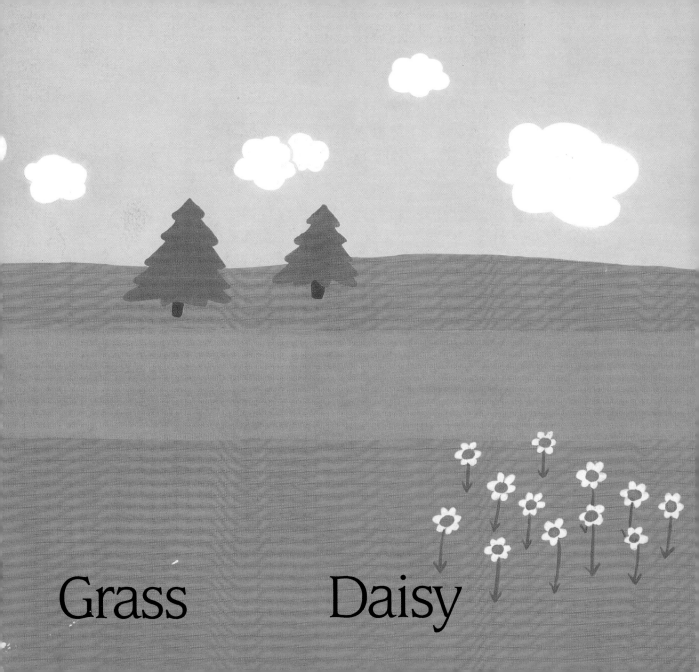

Grass Daisy

Squirrel

Sign

Sun

Sand   Sea   Sail

Umbrella   Towel

Shovel   Pail

Castle

Game

Shell   Boat

Sidestroke   Handstand

Splash   Float

Picnic   Cup

Napkin   Dish

Crab   Gull

Ant   Fish

Sunset   Watch

Shirt   Comb

Parent   Child

Family...

Home